This epic quest

belongs to

For Mum, Dad, Sarah,
and epic-quest enthusiasts everywhere.

OXFORD
UNIVERSITY PRESS

Great Clarendon Street, Oxford OX2 6DP

Oxford University Press is a department of the University of Oxford.
It furthers the University's objective of excellence in research, scholarship, and education by
publishing worldwide. Oxford is a registered trade mark of Oxford University Press in the UK
and in certain other countries

Database right Oxford University Press (maker)

First published 2015

British Library Cataloguing in Publication

Data available
ISBN: 978-0-19-274294-0 (hardback)
ISBN: 978-0-19-274295-7 (paperback)
ISBN: 978-0-19-274296-4 (eBook)

1 2 3 4 5 6 7 8 9 10

Printed in China

Paper used in the production of this book is a natural, recyclable
product made from wood grown in sustainable forests.
The manufacturing process conforms to the environmental
regulations of the country of origin.

SUPER HAPPY MAGIC FOREST

This story begins in the Super Happy Magic Forest,
where everybody enjoys picnics, fun, and frolics
all year round. This is all because of the
Mystical Crystals of Life.

But the forces of evil were at work. One day, the Mystical Crystals of Life were

STOLEN.

Old Oak, the wisest in all the Super Happy Magic Forest, called an urgent meeting.

This is the work of GOBLINS! Who here is brave enough to journey to Goblin Tower, bring back the crystals, and save us all?

Five heroes were chosen. Everybody agreed that they were the bravest warriors in all the land.

With barely enough time to pack a picnic,
the heroes began their epic quest.

They battled through frozen tundras, against cunning and fearsome creatures.

They conquered dungeons that tested their skills to the limit.

The heroes stopped for a picnic, but still
the enemies kept coming.

With their foes defeated, the epic quest
to Goblin Tower was resumed.

At last our heroes arrived at the very
doorstep of evil: Goblin Tower. The fate
of the Super Happy Magic Forest was
in their hands . . . and hooves.

At the Super Happy Magic Forest, the residents were called to another urgent meeting.

FROLIC!